Dedicated to the children
of Dabrowka school

Copyright © 1992 by Nord-Süd Verlag AG, Gossau Zürich, Switzerland
First published in Switzerland under the title *Die Arche Noah*
English translation copyright © 1992 by Rosemary Lanning

First published in the United States, Great Britain, Canada,
Australia and New Zealand in 1992 by North-South Books,
an imprint of Nord-Süd Verlag AG, Gossau Zürich, Switzerland.

Distributed in the United States by North-South Books Inc., New York.

Library of Congress Cataloging-in-Publication Data
Wilkoń, Piotr.
[Arche Noah, English]
Noah's Ark / by Piotr Wilkoń; illustrated by Józef Wilkoń.
Translation of: Die Arche Noah.
Summary: Retells the Old Testament story of how Noah and his
family built the ark and saved the animals from the Great Flood.
ISBN 1-55858-158-8 (trade binding)
ISBN 1-55858-159-6 (library binding)
1. Noah's ark—Juvenile literature.   2. Deluge—Juvenile
literature.   3. Noah (Biblical figure)   4. Bible stories,
English.—O.T. Genesis.   [1. Noah (Biblical figure)   2. Noah's ark.
3. Bible stories—O.T.]   I. Wilkoń, Józef, ill.   II. Title.
BS658.W5313   1992
222'.1109505—dc20   92-2887

British Library Cataloguing in Publication Data
Wilkoń, Piotr
Noah's Ark
I. Title   II. Lanning, Rosemary
III. Wilkoń, Józef
833.914   [J]
ISBN 1-55858-158-8

1 3 5 7 9 10 8 6 4 2
Printed in Belgium

NOAH'S ARK
PIOTR & JÓZEF WILKOŃ

TRANSLATED BY ROSEMARY LANNING

NORTH-SOUTH BOOKS

NEW YORK

Noah woke with a start. A loud rumble had disturbed his sleep. Was it a voice? Or was it thunder? Noah rubbed his eyes sleepily.

"I was dreaming," he told the dove, "of thunder, lightning, and endless rain." He put his hands to his head as more and more of his dream came back to him.

He, his family and hundreds of frightened animals had been crowded into an ark, tossing on a stormy sea.

"A terrible flood is coming and it will cover the whole world!" said Noah. "God is angry with us!" Then he heard the rumble again. A voice boomed: "… an ark, Noah, an ark!"

Noah jumped to his feet. "Quickly!" he said to the dove. "Go and find as many animals as you can. Tell them we have to build an ark, or we will all drown!"

The animals started work at once. Elephants, camels, apes and tigers all came to help. Noah and his sons began to build the ark, and the women gathered food.

Only the hippopotamus refused to help. "Do you really believe in dreams?" he said. "There's not a cloud in the sky. It's not going to rain."

"Don't be stupid, hippopotamus!" said the water buffalo. "Noah knows what he's doing. You'd better come and help."

Noah was sure his dream would come true. He kept urging everyone to work faster. Then he sent the dove out once again, this time to bring back a pair of every kind of animal in the world.

A few days later the sky darkened and the first raindrops fell. The animals stampeded into the ark.

"There's not enough room for all of us!" whined the giraffe.

"Don't tread on my tail feathers!" screeched a peacock.

"Let me go first!" roared the lion.

Noah shooed them all out again. "It's not yet time for you to come on board," he said. "The ark is not ready."

The rain kept falling, and at last the ark *was* ready. Noah and his sons led the animals on board and bedded them down carefully so that they would all fit in. No sooner was the last and smallest animal inside the ark than a tremendous downpour began.

The rain poured down as if all the floodgates in the sky had been opened. And so it went on for days and days and days. Soon the whole earth was flooded and the huge ark tossed on the water like a little nutshell.

"It's a good thing I believed in my dream," said Noah to the dove.

"And that the animals trusted you," she replied.

But it wasn't long before the animals began to grumble. "There's a hole in the roof," complained the apes. "Water keeps dripping on our heads."

"Be quiet," snapped the rhinoceros, "at least it lets some fresh air in."

"The ceiling's much too low!" wailed the giraffes.

"Quite right!" growled a hippopotamus. "There's hardly room to move. I wish I'd gone somewhere else for help...."

Noah stroked his beard and tried not to lose his temper, but soon he could bear the grumbling no longer.

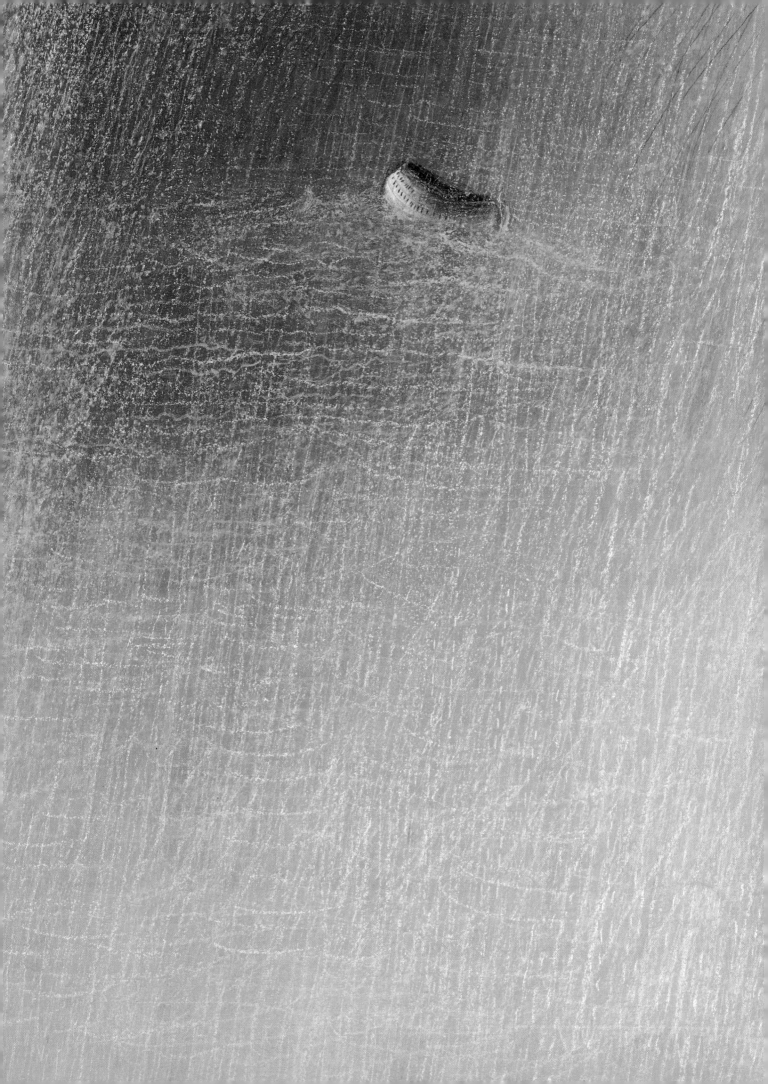

"Just remember," said Noah sternly, "that if I had not taken you into this ark you would all have drowned."

Then the animals were quiet again. They knew that they should be grateful to Noah.

From then on the larks always woke Noah with their sweetest songs; the parrots combed his beard for him; the apes scrubbed the decks; the giraffes stopped grumbling and the hippos shuffled closer together to leave more room for the elephants.

For forty days and nights rain drummed on the roof of the ark. Then Noah opened the hatches and the animals looked out.

"I see the top of a mountain!" roared the tiger. Noah knew that this was Mount Ararat, but he still waited for the rain to stop.

When at last the rain did stop, he said, "We must send out a bird to look for dry land."

"Let me go! Let me go!" twittered all the birds, fluttering round his head. Noah chose the raven.

The raven soon came back with bad news: "There is water everywhere!"

Days passed. Then Noah sent the white dove out. She came back quickly, too. The flood had not yet gone down. Only the bare mountaintops were above the water.

The animals were getting impatient. They began to squabble and complain again. "Noah's dream didn't tell us we'd be tossing around in this ark forever," they muttered.

Another week passed, and Noah sent out the dove again. Suddenly there was great excitement. The dove had come back to the ark with a small olive branch in her beak. Somewhere she must have found trees and dry land.

Noah and his sons lifted the roof off the ark. An endless blue sky stretched overhead, and they saw that the ark would soon run aground.

The animals shouted, "Hooray for Noah!" And the elephant lifted him in the air. There was silence for a moment. The animals muttered amongst themselves and then, all speaking at once, they said, "We're sorry we didn't trust you, Noah!"

Noah just smiled. He had forgiven them long ago. He slowly opened the door and went outside. All the animals crowded round the doorway. They wanted to see the new land, to fly into the forests and run over the meadows.

Now the animals stood on the shore in a long line that stretched all the way to the horizon, and Noah began to count them.

Suddenly he noticed a seal in the water behind him.

"Where did you come from?" he said. "You were not with us in the ark."

"You are old and wise, Noah," said the seal. "More than six hundred years old, they say. But you seem to have forgotten that some animals can swim!"

Noah stroked his beard and smiled. Then he turned back to the others, to make a farewell speech.

"We have been in the ark for many days and nights…" he began, but the baboon interrupted him: "Look, Noah, look!" it screeched, pointing at the mountains. A huge rainbow stretched from the peak of Mount Ararat into the valley below.

Noah stood and gazed at it. Then he said softly, "God has sent the rainbow as a sign that we will never have a Great Flood like this again." Noah was surprised at his own words, but before he could think where they had come from, all the animals were scampering off, towards the rainbow.

Noah wearily turned away and was surprised to see the little seal again. "Why are you still here?" he asked her.

"I want to go to the rainbow too. Will you carry me?"

Noah laughed. He laughed so much that his beard flapped up and down, but he picked up the seal and climbed with her to the top of the mountain.

Then, suddenly, Noah saw a white dove flying over the rainbow. She was coming back to him!

"How could I leave you, Noah," she said, "when you saved my life?"